ALI BABA AND THE FORTY THIEVES

STONE ARCH BOOKS
a capstone imprint

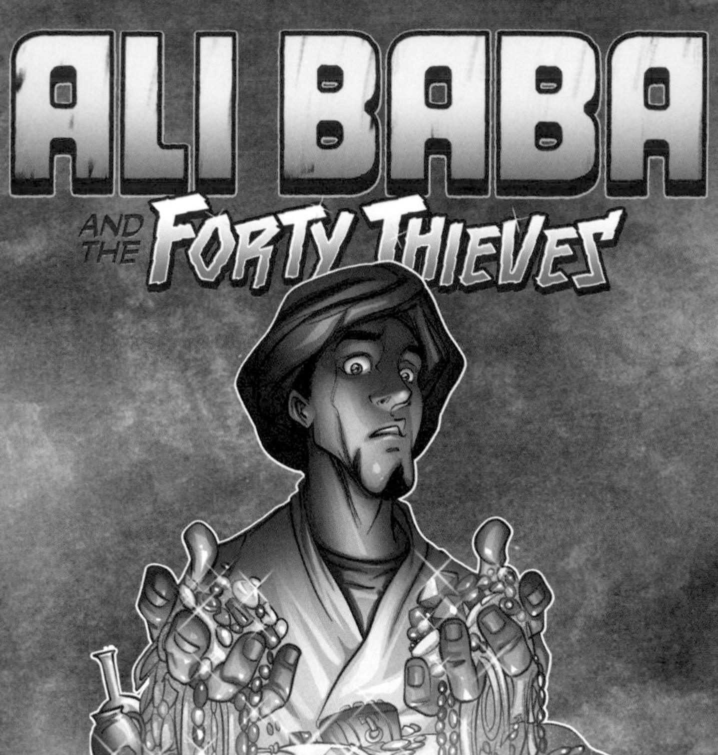

RETOLD BY MATTHEW K. MANNING
ILLUSTRATED BY RICARDO OSNAYA

DESIGNER: BRANN GARVEY
EDITOR: DONALD LEMKE
ASSOC. EDITOR: SEAN TULIEN
ART DIRECTOR: BOB LENTZ
CREATIVE DIRECTOR: HEATHER KINDSETH
EDITORIAL DIRECTOR: MICHAEL DAHL

Published by Stone Arch Books, A Capstone Imprint 151 Good Counsel Drive, P.O. Box 669 Mankato, Minnesota 56002 www.capstonepub.com

Cataloging-in-Publication Data is available on the Library of Congress website.

ISBN: 978-1-4342-1988-6 (library binding)
ISBN: 978-1-4342-2776-8 (paperback)

Summary: The story of Ali Baba, a young Persian boy who discovers a cave filled with gold and jewels, the hidden treasures of forty deadly thieves. Unfortunately, his greedy brother, Kasim, cannot wait to get his hands on the riches. Returning to the cave, he is captured by the thieves and killed, and now the evil men want revenge on Ali Baba as well.

Printed in the United States of America in Stevens Point, Wisconsin.
072013
007513R

CONTENTS

CAST OF CHARACTERS

KASIM

ALI BABA

ALI BABA'S WIFE

MARJANA

ALI BABA'S SON

THE CAPTAIN . . .

AND HIS 39 THIEVES

CHAPTER ONE:
THE TREASURE CAVE
Long ago, in ancient Persia . . .
Easy, boy! Not much farther.
What are you complaining about?
You think I like collecting firewood all day?
NEIGGGH!
We all can't marry into wealth like my brother, Kasim.
Some of us still work for a living.

RRRRRRRRRRRRRRRRRRRR
Some of us were silly enough to marry for love —
What is that?
RRRRRRRRRRRRR!
Is that . . . a caravan?
Oh no!
RRRRUUUMMMMMBLE!

The thieves are coming!
Move, you stubborn mules!
Hurry! Hurry!
RRRRUMBLE!

If we're spotted, you won't be worrying about firewood anymore . . .

Faster! Faster!
CLOP!
CLOP!
CLOP!
CLOP!
CLOP!

We're here, men!
Unload the cargo, and be quick about it!
Ugh! I'm surprised my horse could carry this load.
Better heavy than light, I say —
Careful!!
That gold's worth more than your life!
SMASH!!

Now let's see how the rest of our treasure is faring . . .
OPEN SESAME!!
KKRRRRRRRRR!
Oh my!

All right, men, let's move!
The day's not done yet!!
You heard the captain, boys.
Stash the treasure in the cave.
Several hours later . . .
KKRRRRRR
ZZZZZZZZ
Huh —? What was that?

Good work, men. Mount up!
We need to hurry if we want to reach the city of Susa by nightfall.
Oh, yes . . .

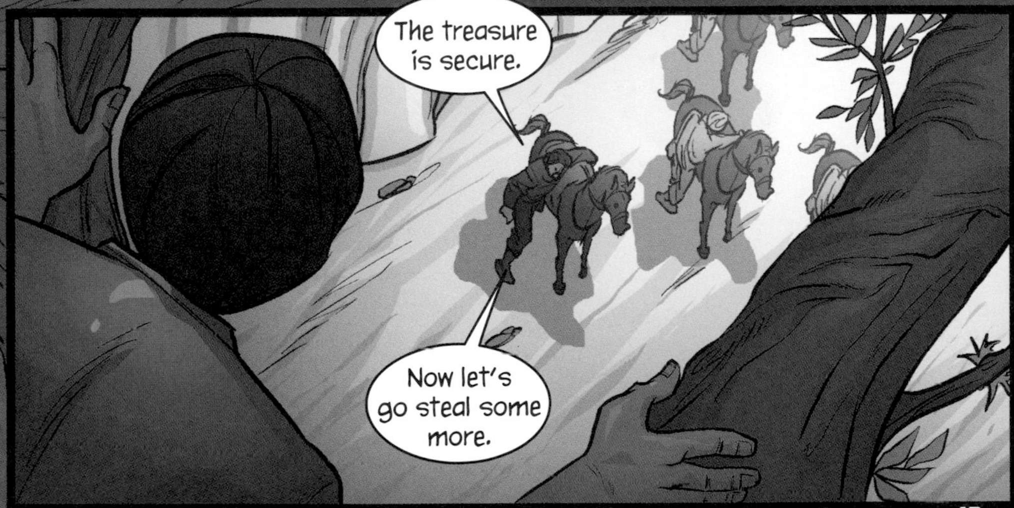

We won't have time to stop to –
What was that?
NEIGH!
Wait.

Quiet, men!
Oh no! 
Never mind.
We're off!

Whew! That was close.
I should be safe now.
But I must hurry before they return.

What did that captain say again?
Open . . . sesame?
RUMMMMMMBLE!

Look at all this treasure!
The thieves would kill me if they caught me here.
I must hurry!
I'll take as much as the mules can carry . . .

. . . and never return.
I almost forgot . . .
NEIGGGHHH!
Close sesame!
Now hurry home, boys.
Before those thieves catch us.

CHAPTER TWO:
A FAMILY AFFAIR
Later that night . . .
Treasure? You should be ashamed of yourself!
Don't worry, dear!
The men I took this from won't even know it's missing.
But it's blood money!
No, it's our money now.
This treasure is the answer to our prayers.

Do you even know how much is here?
Just out of curiosity, I mean.
Enough.
I'm going to bury it in the yard, while it's still dark.
We should know the exact amount, Ali Baba.
I'll go to your brother's and borrow a scale.
I don't think Kasim should know about this —
I won't tell him what the scale is for . . .
I promise.

The next morning . . .
KNOCK!
KNOCK!
KNOCK!

So how much gold is left in the cave?!
Sigh! Come in, Kasim.

My wife told you?
Surely you'll share your findings, Ali Baba?

Don't you have enough money already?
Haven't I taught you anything, little brother . . . ?

. . . You can always spend more money.
Where are you hiding it?
I'll tell you, brother . . .
". . . but you must keep it a secret."
Here's the tree Ali Baba told me about . . .

. . . And this must be the secret entrance!
I hope I can remember the password . . .
. . . Open sesame?!
RRRRRUMBLE!
Unbelievable!
I didn't bring enough mules to carry it all!

Where shall I even begin?
This looks like as good of place as any.
But then . . .
The door! It closed behind me!
Let's see, what was the password?
Open barley?

Open . . . saffron?

Open cinnamon?
Open safflower?!

What was it? I can't . . .

I can't . . .
TIsSSs

I can't remember!
Ali Baba!!

Meanwhile, Ali Baba buried his own treasure . . .
Father? Someone's knocking at the door.
See who it is, my son. I'm almost finished out here.
KNOCK! KNOCK!
I'm coming.
Oh, is your . . . is Ali Baba at home?

Marjana? Is everything all right?
Sorry it's so late, but my master, Kasim, hasn't returned home tonight.
You're the only family he has since his wife passed.
Don't worry, Marjana. I know where Kasim was headed.
I'll leave tomorrow evening when it's safer.
Safer?! Is Master Kasim in danger?
If he is, Marjana, the fault is mine.

A day later, Kasim remained trapped . . .
RUUUMBLE!
!
Who's there?
FWUMP!
Ali Baba, is that you?
Unload the cargo, and be quick about it!

Oh no! The thieves Ali Baba warned me about!
They have returned!!
OPEN SESAME!!
Hmm . . . Something doesn't feel right.

Ahh!!
Huh?

Oof!
I did it! I'm free!
Uh-oh.

Get him!!

No, please!! I'll give it all back! I'll —

A few hours later . . .
RUSTLE!
RUSTLE!
RUSTLE!

What was that?

You're one of Kasim's, aren't you? But where is he –?

The cave! It's closed!
Kasim?

Kasim are you –?
Oh no . . . blood.

Open sesame!
KKRRRRRP

Kasim!!

CHAPTER THREE:
A NECESSARY PLAN
WHAP! WHAP!
WHAP!
I'm sorry, Marjana. Kasim is . . . He's . . .
Oh my!
Take his body around to the garden, Ali Baba.
I'll make arrangements in the morning.

The next day . . .
It's done.
I told the doctor that Kasim was very ill.
He gave me this medicine.
In a few days, I'll inform him that it didn't work.
He'll think Kasim died from his illness —
But his body . . . it's —

That's why we'll need a tailor.
What would we need a tailor for?
To, um, sew the body back together for the funeral.

Meanwhile, at the cavern . . .
Good ride, men.

Let's see how our visitor is keeping, shall we?

OPEN SESAME!!

?
Where is he?!

I thought I told you to stake his body to the wall!
We did, Captain!

Then it appears we've had another intruder . . .
. . . and he didn't take our little warning to heart.

Unload your treasures, men! We're headed to the city.
Someone there must know what happened to the body.

After all, the funeral couldn't have been very pleasant.

Later that day . . .
Excuse me. Have you witnessed any funerals in the city lately?
No.

How about you, boy. Seen anything unusual?
No, sir.

I don't know what you're talking about.

This is useless —
Wait! Listen . . .
I'm telling you, friend, this was the strangest job I've ever had . . .

The poor man had been cut right in half!

Gruesome work, but it needed doing just the same.

!

After all, I'm just a tailor. They pay me to stitch, not to judge.

You hear something?

The next day, at Kasim's house . . .

I'm glad you're all moving in here.

I was getting lonely without Kasim.
Yes, I think it's for the best.

Is that everything, Marjana?
Yes, Ali Baba. Thank you.

I just hope Father feels the same.

Meanwhile . . .
Is that all of them?
Yes, Captain.
But why did you want us to bring out the oil jars?
Get in, and I'll show you!
But, Captain —

Are you questioning my orders?!
N-n-no, sir. I mean, Captain.
Good! Then get in!
And the rest of you do the same!
That tailor was kind enough to tell us the whereabouts of our little intruder.
". . . And I think we should pay him a surprise visit."

CHAPTER FOUR:
DINNER GUESTS
That night . . .
May I help you?
Sorry to bother you, sir, but I've been traveling all day.
Is there any place to stay around here?

Come inside and warm yourself.
My wife is away, and it'll be nice to have someone to talk with at dinner.
You can leave your horses and oil jars in the stable.

Well, thank you. This is all just . . . too kind.

Marjana, Father says there's going to be one more for dinner.
But I was almost done cooking.
Don't blame the messenger. Father invited some oil man in for the night.
And now the lamp's out! Eating in the dark surely won't impress our guest.
Why not borrow some oil from one of our guest's jars?
That's not a bad idea.
Mind the fire, will you?

A few moments later . . .
What is an oil man doing with forty horses?
I'll just take enough oil for the lamps.
!
Is it time, Captain?

Ah!
Captain? Are you all right?
You said you'd signal us with stones when we're ready to attack.
Of course. Stick to the plan.
I just needed a little oil.
Only the marked jar has oil. Remember, Captain.

Of course.
This should be plenty.

That's
a lot of oil,
Marjana!

You know
he might notice
that you took
so much.

Hey,
are you all
right?
How did
they find
us?

Marjana?
Tell me
when the oil
is boiling, will
you?

Soon . . .
This is for Kasim!
Ah!! Noooo!
SSSSSSSSSS

Afterward . . .
Marjana, do you plan to keep our guest waiting much longer?
I just finished heating things up, Ali Baba.
Wonderful! Is there any place I could wash a bit first?
Oh, certainly. There's a basin next to the courtyard.
Thank you again, Ali Baba.

You've been most generous this evening.
Outside . . .
Now to begin our attack!
Time to wake up the troops.
FLING!

TINK!
TINK!
TINK!
What's wrong? Why aren't they —?
Sir, dinner is about to be served.
I was just on my way to wash up before —
Oh, there's no time for that now, sir.
You don't want your soup to get cold, do you?

Moments later . . .

You sure we haven't met before? You look familiar.
No, I think I would remember.

But that reminds me. Perhaps I should check on my horses, if you don't mind –

Gentlemen! If I may have your attention!

For your entertainment, the house of Ali Baba now presents the 1,001 dances of Marjana the Majestic!
Is it all right, Father?
Ha ha! Oh course, my son. It's a fine idea.
You're in for a treat now. Our little Marjana is quite the dancer.
Well, I guess one dance . . .

. . . couldn't hurt.

Ahh!
SCHIIING!

What have you done?! Have you lost your mind, girl?
Go look in the oil jars!

EPILOGUE:
THE WEDDING DAY
Just beautiful, wasn't she?
Rumor has it she saved his life.
I can't believe she used to be a servant girl.

So happy we could make it, my dear.
What was that song they played earlier?

Excuse me for a minute, sweetheart.

There you are, Father. We were looking for you.
And I, you. I wanted to give you my wedding gift.
Your stubborn mule?

No, my son. This gift carries much more weight.
What is it, Father?
A simple phrase . . .
"Open sesame."

The story of "Ali Baba and the Forty Thieves" is part of a collection of Middle Eastern and South Asian folktales known as *One Thousand and One Nights.* These tales have been passed down from generation to generation for hundreds of years. The first English-language edition, titled *The Arabian Nights' Entertainment,* was published in 1706.

Since then, many versions of the book have been published — some containing more than 1,000 stories. In each of these editions, the tales of mystery and adventure are told by the same narrator, a beautiful woman named Scheherazade. She has just married an evil ruler who plans to kill her before the night is through. To stop him, Scheherazade entertains the king with a new story each night, and he soon forgets about his deadly plan.

The Arabian Nights tales remain some of the greatest stories ever told. They include popular adventures, such as "The Fisherman and the Genie," "The Seven Voyages of Sinbad," and "Ali Baba and the Forty Thieves." Many of these stories have been adapted into movies, books, and plays that are still popular today.

REAL HIDDEN TREASURES

In 1520, Spanish explorer Hernando Cortes and his men raided the Aztec empire, stealing the treasure of their emperor, Montezuma. Before the Spanish crew could escape, the Aztecs attacked, and the jewels were spilled and buried around Lake Tezcuco, near modern day Mexico City. Despite many efforts, these treasures have never been found.

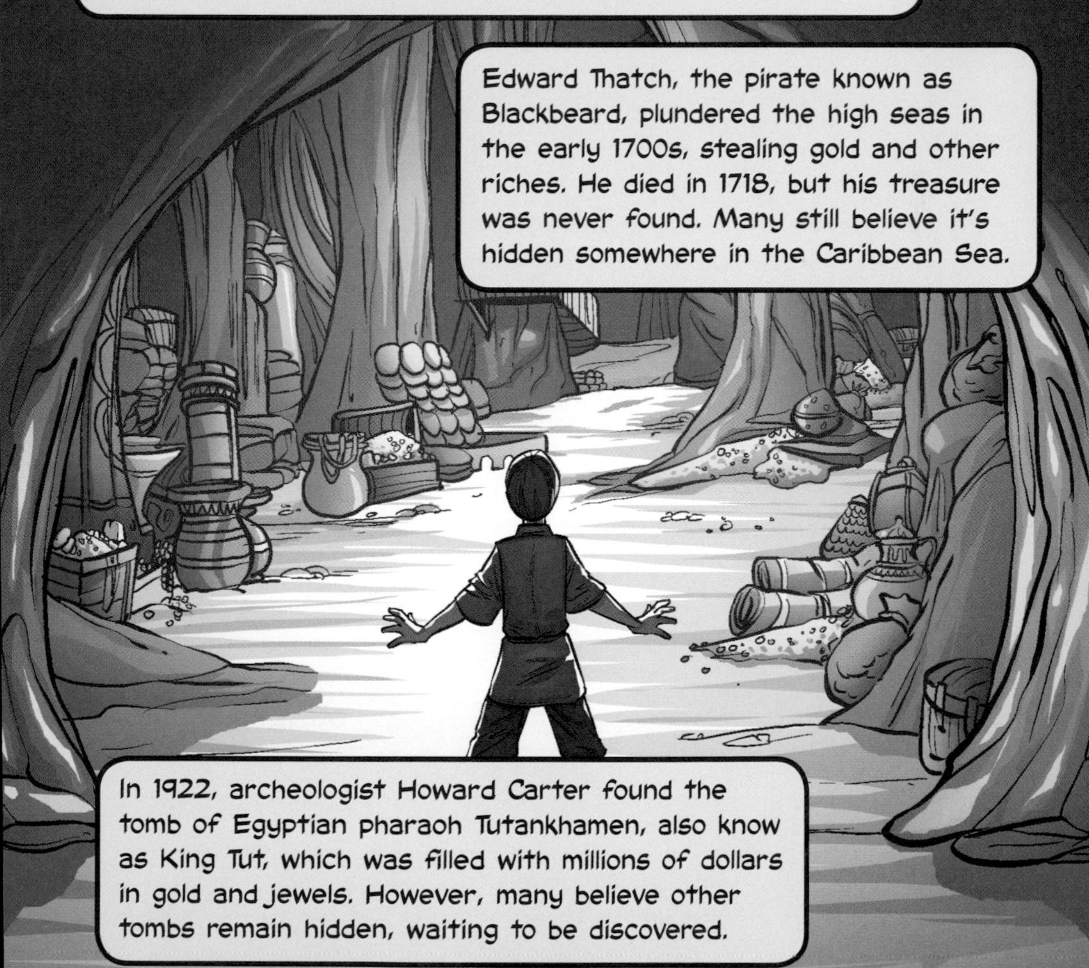

Edward Thatch, the pirate known as Blackbeard, plundered the high seas in the early 1700s, stealing gold and other riches. He died in 1718, but his treasure was never found. Many still believe it's hidden somewhere in the Caribbean Sea.

In 1922, archeologist Howard Carter found the tomb of Egyptian pharaoh Tutankhamen, also know as King Tut, which was filled with millions of dollars in gold and jewels. However, many believe other tombs remain hidden, waiting to be discovered.

ABOUT THE AUTHOR

Matthew K. Manning is a comic book writer, historian, and fan. Over the course of his career, he's written comics or books starring Batman, Superman, Iron Man, Wolverine, Spider-Man, the Incredible Hulk, the Legion of Super-Heroes, the Justice League, and even Bugs Bunny. Some of his more recent works include DK Publishing's *Marvel Chronicle* and Running Press's *The Batman Vault*. He is currently writing a mini-series for the DC Comics imprint Wildstorm. He lives in Brooklyn, New York, with his wife Dorothy and a baby girl on the way.

ABOUT THE ILLUSTRATOR

Ricardo Osnaya is a self-taught illustrator, living and working in Mexico. Since first publishing editorial illustrations in *Excelsior Magazine*, Osnaya has made a name for himself as a freelance artist. He's published the comics *Burundis* and *Dos Guerreros* and illustrated popular characters, such as the Power Rangers. Currently, Osnaya collaborates with Protobunker Studio and works as a comic and illustration instructor at the Mexican Institute of Youth and other schools.

arrangement *(uh-RAYNJ-muhnt)*—plans for something to happen, such as a funeral service

basin *(BAY-suhn)*—a large bowl used for washing

caravan *(KA-ruh-van)*—a group of people or vehicles traveling together

cargo *(KAR-goh)*—freight that is carried by some form of transportation, such as a mule

cavern *(KAV-ern)*—a large cave

courtyard *(KORT-yard)*—an open area surrounded by walls

curiosity *(kyur-ee-AHSS-i-tee)*—an eagerness to find out

gruesome *(GROO-suhm)*—disgusting or horrible

inform *(in-FORM)*—to tell someone something

intruder *(in-TROOD-uhr)*—a person who forces their way into a place where they are not wanted

secure *(si-KYOOR)*—safe, firmly closed, or well protected

sesame *(SESS-uh-mee)*—a small oval seed, which comes from a tropical plant

stubborn *(STUHB-urn)*—hard to deal with

tailor *(TAY-lur)*—someone who makes or alters clothes

DISCUSSION QUESTIONS

1. Ali Baba stole from the thieves because he needed money for his family. Do you think stealing is ever right? Explain your answer.

2. Marjana kills the evil captain. She believes this action is the only way to protect herself and her family. Do you think her decision was okay? Why or why not?

3. At the end of the story, Ali Baba tells his son the secret password to the treasure cave. Do you think Ali Baba's son will use the password to get more riches? Explain.

WRITING PROMPTS

1. Write a final chapter to this book. What happens next? Does Ali Baba's son go back to the cave? Do the authorities ever find out about the missing thieves? You decide.

2. If you had a cave full of treasure, what would you buy? Write a story describing how you would use the riches.

3. Imagine your own Arabian Nights tale. Think of a story filled with mystery and adventure. Then write it down and read it to friends and family.

ARABIAN NIGHTS TALES

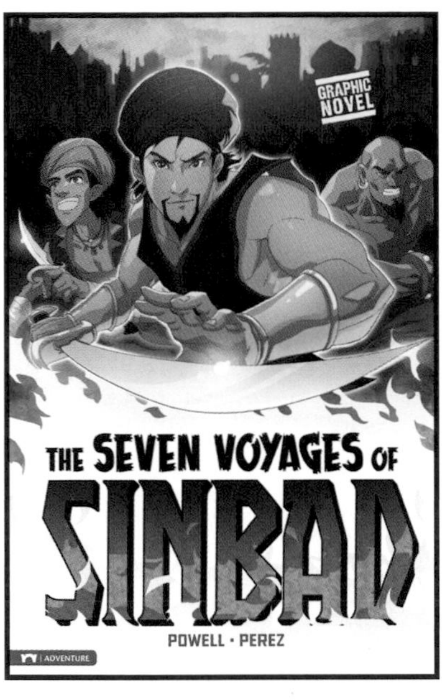

THE SEVEN VOYAGES OF SINBAD

The tale of Sinbad the Sailor, who goes to sea in search of great riches and discovers even greater adventures. On his seven treacherous voyages, the Persian explorer braves a shipwreck, fights off savage cannibals, and battles a giant Cyclops, hoping to survive and tell his legendary story.

THE FISHERMAN AND THE GENIE

The legendary tale of an evil Persian king, who marries a new wife each day and then kills her the next morning. To stop this murderous ruler, a brave woman named Scheherazade risks her own life and marries the king herself . . . but not without a plan. On their wedding night, she will entertain him with the tale of the Fisherman and the Genie — a story so amazing, he'll never want it to end.

WAIT!
DON'T close the book!
There's MORE!
www.capstonekids.com
Still want MORE?
Find cool websites and more books like this one at www.Facthound.com
Just type in the Book ID: 9781434219886
and you're ready to go!